HONEYBONES

HONEYBONES
GEORGINA BRUCE

First published 2020 by TTA Press

ISBN 978-1-9163629-1-8

A CIP catalogue record for this book is available from the British Library

Proofread by Peter Tennant

Designed and typeset by the publisher

TTA Press
5 Martins Lane
Witcham
Ely
Cambs CB6 2LB
UK

ttapress.com
shop.ttapress.com

Printed and bound in the UK by 4edge Ltd

FOR THE ENDLESS GIRLS

AFTER THE FUNERAL, we came back home to the house of mirrors.

%

The day of the funeral seemed to start at the end, when the front door slammed, and the girls in the mirrors slipped away like silverfish, out of sight through doors and windows and around corners, into the house inside the house. It was a house of mirrors, and it was entangled with its selves, a pattern looping inwards, up stairs and through doorways and round corners, round and round and up and down. That day the houses had locked together. The real house and the house of mirrors. Fused at the spine. Tangled at the teeth. Knotted at the hair.

Three mirrors watched each other in the hallway. I watched the girls in the mirrors. The endless girls, faces shining with rain and blood. Their mouths were crooked and their cheeks were bruised. They ate me with their eyes. They ate without moving their lips, a sound like crashing glass, slow-motion glitter-smash, a sparkle of blood.

I was not alone in the house. I heard my mother behind me. Water raining from her hair and clothes. I imagined her black-shod feet, her boots soft with water, the pools of rain running over the tiles. She was behind me, on the stairs, making a sound like she was crashing her wings. I kept my eyes on the endless girls in the mirror. I wanted to close my eyes but then they could take me. *Into the under the house.* To the house inside the house. What if they already had?

Tom warned us not to stand in the hallway where the mirrors criss-crossed, and now I knew why. He told us not to get lost in a dream, for our own good. *No dreaming in the house of mirrors.* That was the rule.

But Mum had come to me in secret and whispered, *if you want to dream, go into the garden where you won't be bothering anyone.*

It was already too late, too late for that.

The front door slammed and the day started again.

%

Anna, you are dreeming.

%

My mother rained water from the hem of her black silk dress, from her long hair, from her pale fingertips. Her dress clung to her like skin, and her bones shone through her skin like hard moons. She staggered by me in a haze of bleach and perfume.

"Mum?"

Her face pinched tight into a bud of silence. She went up the stairs in a strange, agonised manner, bone by scraping bone. Gripping the banister so her knuckles glistened. Her legs buckled but she went on. At the top of the stairs, where she thought I couldn't see, she drooped to her knees and then fell slowly forward onto her face.

I was watching her in the mirror as she crawled out of sight.

Then Tom was there.

"We make a handsome pair," he said.

My black satin dress had a full skirt and puffed sleeves that made me feel like an overgrown infant. Tom wore a black suit of very fine cashmere; so soft that when you touched it, it almost wasn't there. His long hands looked very white. He smelled of vanilla, as though he'd been baking a cake.

"What shall we do about you, eh, Anna?"

I forced out a shrug. I couldn't speak because the sound of my voice in my head was so stupid, like a braying duck, making no sense. I didn't understand what was happening. Tom's breath smelled of instant coffee and it sent me spiralling into my head. There was an eruption, a familiar roar of laughter. It echoed from wide open mouths as I ran past the staffroom, red mouths dripping over a magazine. Their eyes flicked up and caught me at the exact moment I looked in through the half-open door. I saw what they were doing. A glossy page spread open before their soft hanging faces. I knew what it was. Their laughter followed me down the corridor. It filled me with shame, though I didn't know why. It had nothing to do with me; she had nothing to do with me. Whoever was spread out before them with a staple through her seam. On the back of the toilet door, the familiar message was scratched out in biro. *Anna Carrow is a slag.* Then capital letters BITCH in fresh black felt tip. I didn't know why they had started, these messages. Ever since we moved into the house, school was like this. Like they hated me. Like they all knew something I didn't.

But Tom said it was fine. Tom said I never had to go back.

Tom was an artist; he didn't think the way other men thought. He was rich and didn't need to follow everyone else's rules. And once he'd told me I was beautiful. I was fourteen that day, it was my fourteenth birthday. The day he'd said I was beautiful.

"Come on, Dolly Daydream." He put his hand in my hair, in the mass of it at the back of my head. I was shivering with cold; it was always cold in the house. I had the sensation of looking at myself from a very long way away. As if I wasn't really there. The two of us, side by side in the mirror. His long white hand in my hair. My dress looked so strange to me; it almost felt as if someone else was wearing it, or that the act of wearing it made me someone else.

"Time to tango," said Tom.

The front door slammed and the day started again.

%

Mum went to bed and locked the bedroom door and wouldn't speak to me at all, not even through the wall. When it grew dark, I switched on the lights, one by one, trailing my hands over cold wallpaper. I knocked softly on Mum's door. "Aren't you hungry? Don't you want anything? Are you warm enough? Shall I make you a cup of tea?"

Her response was a deeper and harder silence.

I left her and ran back through the house to my own room, along the landing and up the twisted corner stairs to a little door, then several deep steps down in the dark to a door at the bottom, which opened onto a long white corridor. My breath was visible in the air and my teeth were shaking. It was always colder on this side of the house. There was a door at the far end which opened into my bedroom. Between the staircase door and my bedroom were eleven other doors, six to the left and five to the right. I hesitated. Ever since we'd moved into the house, the doors had been locked shut. But today I saw they were each ajar.

When is a door not a door?

Tom didn't like me going into rooms without his permission, but the open doors felt like an invitation. I pushed the first door. It silently slid over carpet, peeled away to reveal a child's bedroom. Large and empty but for a bed, a toy box, a rocking horse by the window. I went towards the rocking horse but the air froze before me, and I found myself pushing against it. A noise was leaking from the air, the sound of a voice clicking and echoing inside a stone. I lifted the lid of the toy box, and saw a leg sticking out from among a jumble of plastic bricks and threadbare teddies. I pulled it up by its foot, and out came a child-sized doll, four feet tall. She had blonde plastic ringlets and wore a pink nylon dress with puffed sleeves and cheap white trim on the hem of the skirt.

She spoke with a mechanical voice, a broken slur and click between each word.

come and play with me!

come into the under the house

it's a dreemy world for dreemy peeple

come into the under the house

What was that supposed to mean? Come into the under the house?

I opened the Velcro strip on its dress. There was a cord hanging out of the plastic casing in the middle of its back. In the centre of its chest, a heart-shaped logo was moulded into the plastic and the words *Dreemy Peeple* branded next to it in flowery cursive. And then there was the little patch of holes in the stomach for the Dreemy Peeple's speaker, a robotic voice cranking out its lines.

come and play with me!

let's go dancing all night long

come into the under the house

it's a dreemy world for dreemy peeple

What did that even mean? It made no sense. *Come into the under the house.* I let go of the doll and it fell forwards on its face, reciting its lines into the carpet.

I opened the next door. The room was very similar, and I began to think of boarding schools and dormitories. Didn't Mum tell me this house used to be a school, once upon a time? Or did she say a sanatorium? A hospital? This room didn't have a rocking horse, but there was a bookcase stuffed full with books, and I felt a surge of longing for them. My books had gone missing in the move, and I wasn't allowed to touch the books in the library yet; they were too precious and ancient and full of things too grown up for me (or so Tom thought). But here, this room had its own bookcase full of books. I stood before it and ran my fingers over the leather spines. The books felt cold. Refrigerated. They were ancient, and not in good condition. I couldn't make out the titles: they were too faded to read or the letters were unrecognisable to me. One book looked ruined; the spine had completely crumbled away from the pages. I pulled it from the shelf. My fingers were numb from cold, too rubbery to turn the pages. But I didn't need to: the book fell open to a natural groove, and lay flat in my hands. Falling apart there as though this were the page everyone wanted, this, the heart of it all. Words written here on thin dirty paper.

They want to speak with their own mouths, and move their own tongues against their own teeth. They want to be wild creatures making noises from their bellies, or singing high through the tight wet cords of their throats. They want to make laughter from the pit of themselves, uncontrolled and unashamed. All night, all through the day, they want to groan and sigh, to grunt like animals, as fingers and tongues work them from below. They want. So much. Their dreams are loud. They fill bedrooms with madness, magic tricks, vases of reeking flowers, garish vanity, their long hair matted in the paddle brush. One hundred strokes before bed. A dirty joke. Fuck me harder. Harder. No...too hard. No, stop it. Push away your hands, they try to stop you. They bleed on the sheets and towels, blood on thighs, red butterfly stains when they press their legs together. They lock doors against you. They try to run away. They slam pots on the stove, burn toast, burn their hands. Cry cry cry! They weep in the mornings, they sob in the afternoons, they blub all night long. They cry themselves out, they scour themselves out until their insides are cracked and shattered and spat out in pieces: vegetable matter, blood, soil, rubber, ink, dust, hairballs…it all comes up. They eat strange things. You find them in the garden eating dirt, you watch them chew a wine glass at the dinner table. They are emptier than you imagined. You feel yourself straining to fill them, to burst open inside them, drain yourself into their hollows. But it is too tormenting, it only gets worse… You know you are cheating yourself. But you can't help it. You move the clock forward. You bring on the time, snap it towards you like a tablecloth, plates and dishes crashing to the ground. Then all at once it is happening. They are here, in the house, and you—

I jumped. A mechanical clatter had started up behind me. I dropped the book on the rug. On the bed, splayed out with limbs akimbo, a Dreemy Peeple muttered her robotic messages.

come and play with me!

come into the under the house

it's a dreemy dreemy dreemy dreemy dreemy dreemy

She was stuck like a record. I didn't know what to do. I didn't really want to touch her plastic skin. The curls of hair. Her rosebud lips so pink and plush in her baby face. It made me unhappy to look at her and hear her broken voice.

dreemy dreemy dreemy dreemy dreemy

The cord in her back was stuck fast and broken. I couldn't see a battery panel. Surely she would run out of power soon. She was stuttering badly.

dreemy dreemy-my-my-my-my-my

I heard footsteps above me and suddenly felt afraid. What if Tom knew I was in here? In rooms where I did not belong. What if it was my fault the doll had broken? I turned her over so she was speaking into the pillow and her failing stuttered words could barely be heard. My hands were so cold they didn't feel like my hands, and when I touched the Dreemy Peeple, it was like two dolls touching. Plastic and numb.

///

In my own room, I wedged the door closed with a chair under the handle. I was shaking with cold but I had to have the window open or I felt my breath would be stuck in my chest forever. I pushed up the window and put my head out into the rain. It was raining in sheets, a torrent of rain, and my mouth filled with water. I hung my head down and let the rain drool out from my open mouth. It had been raining for weeks. At the funeral, the rain flooded the graveyard. We were sinking into the mud, and everyone's good black shoes were ruined.

Don't think about that.

I would ask Tom about the other rooms. One night when he was in the mood for telling stories. I'd sit by the fire in his library and he'd tell me what those rooms were for. Who the dolls belonged to. Whose books were those? I wouldn't ask him about what I'd read. That would be too embarrassing. Tom was a sensitive man, an artist. He wouldn't want to talk about the things in that book. The grunting and moaning and eating glass for dinner. But the rooms, I would ask him about the rooms. Or maybe I shouldn't ask him about the rooms. Maybe I needed to check that the rooms were still there before I asked him about them. Because what if he said, what rooms? And I'd know it was all my invention. I made it all up in my head.

That's what I did. I saw things the wrong way. I saw things that weren't there. I heard things when they made no sound. Things happened to me which seemed real but they weren't real. They only happened in my head. Things happened to me which were the sorts of things that didn't happen in real life. They were the sorts of things that happened only in the heads of people with *severe mental illnesses*. I repeated such comforting words like a mantra, as if they could explain me to myself. *Schizophrenia, psychosis, delusion...*

Tom realised there was something wrong when me and Mum moved into the house. When the nightmares began, he arranged for me to see Doctor Lumna. She diagnosed anxiety and prescribed drugs with unpronounceable names. Some of the drugs made me sleepwalk and some made me dream. She said they would make me better. And if they didn't, there was always the hospital.

My head hanging out of the window in the rain, rain pouring from my hair. I heard a metallic clank clank clank. I turned my head and lifted my wet hair from my face. There was a shape, long arms and legs climbing up the narrow and ancient fire escape. Moving fast and sure, his hood pulled up over his head. I didn't need to see his face; I knew already it could only be Thew. Oh not now, I thought, and I felt the thought shoot down to him, and felt the rusted metal step beneath him wobble with the weight of his intention.

The fire escape zigzagged near my bedroom window. It was easy enough for Thew to stand on the railing and swing over and into the room. If I moved aside for him. I stayed where I was.

"What do you want?"

"Are you okay?"

"I'm fine."

"Anna!"

I stepped out of the way and Thew climbed up swiftly and was in the bedroom. He was soaked, dripping rainwater into the carpet. I watched it spread darkness around his feet. I kept my face turned away from him, staring down at the floor.

He reached out to touch my arm but I flinched away.

"I know you're not fine. I was worried about you, after today."

I couldn't hide myself from Thew very easily, but now I didn't know what he meant. What he'd seen in me, on this of all days.

"Don't worry about me," I said. "I can take care of myself."

"I know you can. I was just trying to be nice."

"Oh well thanks for the pity party, in that case."

"Anna, what the fuck?" He dipped his head towards me, trying to get a look at my face. I twisted away from him.

He hesitated. "Do you want to come back to mine? Mum's made up a bed for you."

"I've got a bed here."

"So? You stay over all the time."

"It's different now."

"How? Because of us?"

I shrugged and said nothing. I wouldn't look up at him, and I could sense his impatience and incomprehension. He would hate me, he'd think I was a weirdo and want nothing more to do with me. I couldn't tell him. I didn't know what to say to him anymore. It was like he was on the earth and I was on the moon. Like two different dimensions.

I willed him to go away, but he kept standing there. He tried to get me to meet his eyes, but I wouldn't. I stared at the carpet. The damp patch was spreading and I wondered if it would dry by itself, and imagined a little patch of moss growing there.

"Are you going to tell me what happened to your face?"

"Nothing happened to it."

He was silent for a long time, holding me in his attention. At last I felt him relent.

"Well. There's a bed made up for you at mine," he said. I looked up as he turned his back to me and clambered onto the window ledge, dripping mud and rainwater on the wallpaper. He pushed himself out into the air and for a moment I thought he was falling, and imagined him smashed open on the concrete, the rain washing the blood out of his shattered body. But he didn't fall; there was the sound of metal clank and scrape against brick as he caught the railing and vaulted himself over. His movements sent muscles of flame through his body. He landed on all fours, russet and grey, bushy tail sweeping the air. A big red fox ran down the fire escape. No, Thew ran down the fire escape, head down low and not looking back.

%

The night had fallen and the house had fallen, into soft tranquillising beds, not dreaming but sinking into clouds of cotton and silk and feathers, sinking down down down to the dark places, down down into the thick, quiet slumbrous deep. But me: I lay awake and cold, the quilts pulled up around my chin, and listened to the whispers that grew from the silence, the many voices, talking all at once. Chanting and yelling and bribing and wheedling and softly entreating...giving voice to a language I didn't know. To needs and quarrels and stories I had never known. I pressed my head to the pillow, trying not to hear. The voices chanted on, ever louder, the language edging tantalisingly close to meaning. If I could catch one word, I could swing myself up into the rhythm of the speech, I could follow along as it surfed and crested and broke into splinters. Just one tilt of meaning, one tilt towards me, so I could catch on and follow the thread. But it didn't happen and instead the voices ran together, became thick and rope-like, morphed into heavy weights pulling on my arms and legs, a fist in the hair at the back of my head, a hand prying between my legs, hands gripping my ankles, pulling me down. I fought. *I never stopped fighting.* Kicking and thrashing like a beast. I didn't feel afraid; only angry. Enraged and fighting with all my strength. I threw myself out of my body, and saw it hovering six feet above the bed. Kicking and punching the air. *No,* I thought, *no no no.* I snapped back to my body, like a taut string snapping back on itself, and my eyes flew open from terror.

I was awake. I switched on the bedside lamp, searched around for my glasses. The room was still, and silent but for the sound of hard rain. My watch was lost somewhere with my books but I could tell it was late, the middle of the night. The voices were gathering again in the darkness. It was *them,* I realised. It was the Dreemy Peeple. All of them with their cords hanging out of their backs; talking, talking all night long.

I put another jumper on over my pyjamas, pulled on socks and trainers. The doors to the other rooms were all still open. I marched into the room closest to mine and grabbed the Dreemy Peeple doll from where it was lying on the bed.

come and play with me!
    come into the under the house
it's a dreemy world for dreemy peeple
    come into the under the house
come and play with me
i'm your friend
let's go dancing all night long

I dragged it to my room and threw it out of the window. I heard its voice break and the crack of plastic as it hit the metal railing and flopped down onto the concrete below. There were dolls in all the rooms and I did the same with all of them. I dragged them to my room by the hair, two and three in each hand, and flung them out into the rain, their limbs flailing as they plummeted in darkness.

When they were all gone, silence flooded over me. I thought of the Dreemy Peeple all smashed and broken on the lawn. Tom would see them and know it was me who'd done it. Would he be angry? I could claim no knowledge, say I must have been sleepwalking. The drugs made me do things I couldn't remember. He'd feel sorry for me. He cared about me so much...that was one thing I could be sure of. The clouds cleared for a moment and let out a pale little moon. I saw the Dreemy Peeple scattered over grass and concrete. I thought about going and hiding them somewhere, dragging them to the woods maybe. Then the sky darkened and the rain came down harder, and I thought no. Let them stay where they are.

%

No sleep that night. Every time I closed my eyes I felt myself buoyed into the air by invisible hands. Fingers pushing between my thighs. Lashing out with arms and legs, twisting away, bucking and kicking and fighting them off.

I lay awake with my eyes wide open, and wondered. There was a strange, sparkly feeling in the air, which meant Tom was in the library, working. Sometimes he would let me watch him. He would talk to me, his voice warm like syrup melting in a pan, hot and dozy, telling story after story, filling my mind with strange images that melted away as soon as I left the room.

I put my trainers on again, and went quickly along the corridor, not looking in the open doors as I ran past. Up the steep staircase, quietly opening the door at the top and closing it behind me. Then down the little twisted corner steps to the landing. Tom's library was downstairs, off the hallway. The hallway glimmered in the darkness, the mirrors bouncing around a sliver of moonlight shining through the front door. I shut my eyes, afraid of mirrors in the darkness, and navigated by touch until I reached the library door. There was music clamouring in my mind, a fairground melody or a nursery rhyme, but at the library it fell away and I was disoriented by the sudden silence. I pushed the door open a little. Tom was at his desk, leaning back in his chair. His eyes were closed and his hands fallen by his sides. Asleep, I thought. But in the next instant his eyes were open and on me. The door swung wider; I must have pushed it without knowing. A cold thrill travelled from my feet to my hair as he took me in. I was fuzzy and tangled from night terrors and fighting with sleep, and suddenly I felt very afraid, as though I should not have been there at all.

"Anna," he said.

The way he said it. He wasn't angry. It was like he'd been waiting.

A fire was blazing in the hearth, and the room was suffocating hot. I didn't want to go in anymore. I didn't know why I wanted to before. But the fire was so tempting. The library was the only warm room in the house.

"I couldn't sleep," I said. "I'm sorry."

But he smiled. "Anna," he repeated, and this time I felt a thrum of music reverberate through me.

"Are you sleepwalking again, Anna?"

I walked into the library and closed the door behind me. The fire was high and wild, and flames licked out from the hearth. I moved away, towards the bookshelves, stuffed tight with books, ancient and leather-bound and magical-looking.

"No," Tom said. "Don't touch the books."

I dropped my hand which was reaching for one of the volumes before me.

"Why can't I?"

"You're sleepwalking. You'll be disturbed."

I'm already disturbed, I wanted to say. You don't know the things I feel, the things I see and hear inside my mind.

"Wait," he said. He opened his desk drawer and pulled out

a paperback. “I do have one book you’re allowed to see.”

I went to him, excited, acting a little younger than my age. He put the book in my hand, but wouldn’t let go of it himself. We stood with the book softly vibrating between us.

“It’s because of her that you walk in your sleep,” he said. “She put a curse on me.”

I looked down at the book we held between us. I saw the name *Rose* but nothing else. Our hands were hiding the rest of the cover. Tom’s hand touching mine. I looked up. His face was changing, flickering in the firelight. He was handsome, then ugly, then oh so handsome again. His fingers were cold and intense, pressing on mine.

“She’s a monster now, with a face so grotesque it had to be locked away. Her skin is thick and pitted like a shark. Her body sagging and slow. She was beautiful once but she filled her heart with anger and hatred, against me and against all men. And jealousy, bitter jealousy of all I love. She grew ugly and terrible and insane and when she died she refused to rest and instead she now torments me. She is a monster. Do you understand, Anna?”

All the time he’d been talking, I’d been looking into his eyes, watching them change colour, from green to black. His lips moving slightly out of synchronicity with his words. His tongue flickering at the corners of his mouth. His fingers on mine felt like they were trembling.

“I’d get rid of her if I could. An exorcism.”

“Yes.”

“Do you ever think about it, Anna?”

His hand on mine felt strangely weak and soft. I shook my head.

I realised I couldn't feel the book in my hands, but I could still feel Tom's fingers wrapped around mine. Nothing but the tremble of our cold hands moving together. What had happened to the book? Was there ever a book or was it only in my head? It didn't matter: he was touching my hands. It was enough to be loved; he loved me; this was love, wasn't it? His touch, his eyes burrowing under my skin.

"I never think about it, either," he said.

He looked disappointed. I didn't know what we were talking about. A fear was swelling in my chest, a panic about to erupt. What did he mean? What could I say now, to make him happy again?

Nothing.

He dropped my hands and turned away.

"It's been a difficult day for all of us. Me especially. I need to be alone now."

It was only a dream, a night time excursion. I was sleep-walking, walking my dreams. I knew I wasn't there and it wasn't real. But even in my dream, I was filled with anguish for Tom. I crept from the library, humiliated by his rejection and feeling his hurt and pain. He was so unhappy and once again I had failed him. I was too young, I didn't understand the things he was telling me. Running past Mum's bedroom I sent a volley of mental arrows through the door. *Bitch. Cow. Evil bitch. Stupid cow.* But it wasn't her fault. Rose had got to her, possessed her and poisoned her mind. What did Tom want? What did he need? If I could get rid of Rose, he would love me more than anyone. But Rose was not real, she was only a ghost. And Mum was Tom's true love. But how could she be so cruel to him? How could she let Rose take away their happiness? Why was the house of their love so still, so cold and so sad?

%

Mum wouldn't come out of her room. I stood at the door and pressed my ear to the wood, trying to hear her moving around in there. All I could hear was her silence.

She used to sing. Once upon a time. Laugh and sing and drink red wine, and smoke horrible-smelling weed and chatter on the phone to her friends. In the evenings there would be the sound of music played on the record player, and the crash of glasses from the kitchen, and her brash, high-pitched laugh. But since we moved into Tom's house, she said she couldn't think of anything but him. She brought me into her confidence and I was glad about it, but I didn't know what to say, how to speak to her as a friend. She would shave her legs in the bath while I brushed my hair at the mirror. She would say, *this is a dream, such a beautiful dream. I never thought it would happen to me, not really, not in real life.* I could see it, the dream that had settled on her. She grew ever more beautiful, thinner, more luminous, as if everything inside her had begun to glow and glitter and burn up. Her clothes hung from her bones, satin nightdresses that barely covered her, straps that fell from her shoulders – but she didn't care who saw her body, because it was beautiful, and men craved to touch her, and Tom couldn't keep his hands off her, and women were jealous. It made me uncomfortable when she talked about sex; I was a stupid kid who knew nothing about it. *He wants me*, she would say. *It's amazing that he wants me so much. I want him. He wants me.*

That word, *want,* was so embarrassing. It was what it elided. *He wants to fuck me. I want to fuck him. He wants to do things to my body* – things I couldn't even imagine, couldn't picture, didn't want to know. It reminded me of the things they said about me at school, those names I had acquired, which stuck to me like shame. I couldn't peel those names from myself. I loved Tom for understanding how painful it was; I loved him for keeping me out of school and away from the bullies. He must really care about me to do that. And yes, he loved my mother too. He wanted her. I had sometimes heard their noises at night; they sounded like cats, tearing at each other and howling. And in the mornings, sometimes, she had bruises on her neck and arms. But she was proud of her injuries; she stood at the mirror and rubbed arnica gel on them and smiled to herself.

But it was true, what Tom had told me. Mum said the house was haunted. She said she heard a woman moving in the corridors at night, and was afraid. She felt the woman take possession of her body, she said; she'd been strong and fought her out again. But every time it happened, she became weaker. The woman was cruel and ugly and she wanted to make Mum ugly too. She was jealous of her beauty and wanted to strip it all away. The woman was so monstrous, a monstrous woman. Her mouth so terrible, her head so like a shark's, with thick pitted skin and small black eyes; she was so dangerous that her head had been caged. So she couldn't get to anyone with that awful clashing mouth.

She whispers in my ear, Mum said. *She tells me horrible secrets.*

Now when Mum sang, she sang like a wooden toy, like a wind-up bird, like an empty bell. Once upon a time, she'd sung like a broken heart, but I couldn't even remember her voice, how it used to be. The songs she would play all the time in the old house, the familiar, beautiful songs – she never sang those anymore. She sang the songs Tom wrote for her, but I saw him wince as she butchered her way through them. I couldn't understand how she could sing at all with her voice like a tick-tock, like a clanging bell, like a tin bath with the water emptied out of it.

But now I wished for the sound of her voice again. Anything, say anything at all. Please just say something. I called to her, I whispered through the door, but her silence only grew thicker until it was a heavy cloak; and I felt my words were wrapping around her silence and that I was weaving her in webs like a spider does its prey. I was so selfish. It was all for me. All this trying. My love for her had worn away to a stub of desperation. I sank down onto the floor outside her room, hating her because I needed her. Hating myself for needing her and being too stupid and ugly and worthless to get her love. And I was afraid. Where was she in all that silence? What had Rose done to her?

I went looking for Rose all the time. Over and over, I went looking. Avoiding the library and the rooms downstairs, I kept to the upper levels, the corridor where Mum's room was, and the rooms above that. No matter how I explored, I never quite understood how the wings of the house intersected together. There were always new rooms to find, new passages I hadn't known before. I'd follow a narrow corridor and find myself in the kitchen. Or I'd go through a door I'd never seen and come out in the hallway by the library. Roaming around the house I felt as though I was air, thin air poured into the shape of a girl. Like I was the ghost. I lost sense of time.

I went all over the house and could not seem to exhaust it. Sometimes I saw myself in other rooms. I saw myself writing, hunched over a desk. I saw myself sleeping, splayed out on a bed. I saw myself in mirrors, bloodstained and broken, sliding away away away into the house inside the house, slipping away

away

away

away awash washing water sloshing… I was on a bed and it was rocking, tilting from side to side, water splashing over me, dragging at the sheets… Cold black water. Water lapped up over my feet, and pulled at my skin. And I knew there was something with me in the water, shark-like and scenting my blood. The bed was sinking… I tipped myself out of it as quietly as I could and found my knees scraping hard ground. I quickly stood, up to my waist in water. The water was black and viscous but there was a shell of grey light over me, and I made out a shore ahead, an island with trees of sparkling crystal.

And then the woman was before me.

She was several feet away, standing in water up to her shoulders. I didn't scream or make a sound because I knew that I would die, that she would dart to me through the water and claw me to death with horrible hands. Yet all I could see was her head, shut inside a rusted cage, a head that was pointed and grey like a shark. I was grateful for the cage at least. If she opened her mouth I knew I would see rows of sharp teeth. I was moving closer to her, we were moving together as though the ground itself were moving; it was inevitable now that she would have to devour me. But when I was close enough to see her eyes, they were wild. She tried to speak, but the only sound she could make was a keening, tongueless cry. The cage had a metal bar that pierced the flesh of her cheeks, holding down a flat metal plate that protruded from her mouth. Why did it have to be so cruel? And yet, *she* was cruel, wasn't she? She would not let us have any peace.

I began to understand that there was something she wanted from me. She held up her ancient hands, and with fingers bent and clawed, wrote something in water on her palm. We were too close now: I knew if she touched me I would die, and I panicked, trying to get away, flailing my arms and legs in a fury of water, fighting my own flesh to get away from her, away away away

away in the slipping silver of the mirror

through the door and back in the house, in the hallway where the three mirrors reflected all. I'd seen Rose and survived. But she would come for me, soon. When she'd finished eating my mother's flesh from her bones.

%

Me and Mum, side by side in the mirror. Me in my black satin puffed sleeve dress, and she in her long black slip and high heels, ruined by rain and mud. White flesh streaked with dirt. Her hands twisting in her wet hair. We were not alike, no. But we were the same, exactly the same.

"Mum," I said. But she couldn't hear me. She was caught in her reflection, pinned there, a shimmer in the eye of the house. Her dress stuck to her bones. As beautifully thin and broken as ever. More broken, and thinner than ever. Her long bones made geometric shapes of her. There were no curves anymore, only angles. I envied her, although she was painful to look at. I wanted the pain. Beauty was pain: the bowed spine, rigid shoulders, pale skin draped over her ribcage, sinking between the bones.

i am the queen of knives
and the queen of mouths
and the queen of shadows

She sang without moving her lips.

shadows for eating
mouths for haunting
knives for beauty

The wrong words. What a terrible hymn she was singing to herself.

"Are you alright, Mum?"

i am the queen of mirrors
mirrors for eating

I pulled her hand, tried to drag her away from her reflection. She slapped at me, batting away the air, my hands, my presence. Her eyes fixed on the mirror the whole time.

"Look at me."

But she wouldn't look. She fell into her eyes, falling over and over, endless repetitions of a fall. Her model figure in an angular pose, over and over, almost as though she were nothing but the layering of an image on top of itself, images layered together to give the illusion of depth and movement. She was shallow and distant as a photograph. Why wouldn't she even look at me?

"She's rehearsing." Tom's voice came from above our heads. I span around. He was on the stairs above the hallway, looking down. His cashmere suit so fine and black it almost wasn't there.

"She's practising for her part," he said. "She's really wonderful."

I looked back at my mother. Her image fractalled, multiplied, spiralled outwards in mirror after mirror. The mirror mothers crowded around her; ate her with their eyes.

"Mum, please. I really need you."

She blinked and side-snapped a glimpse of my face.

"I'm not your mother," she said.

She smiled, and it was brutal, a tyrannical smile. A slice of red lipstick opening and stretching. Her voice trembled faintly under the glass.

And go outside if you want to dream. No dreaming in the house of mirrors.

%

I ran down the steep slope of lawn, the grass giving way to mud under my feet. Slipping and sliding to the end of the garden, through the trees and into the woods. The rain eased off a little as I ran away from the house and among the familiar trees. I didn't come outside to dream; I came outside to be awake. To think. I needed my thoughts to run clearly, to understand what was real.

She was rehearsing? How?

What was this play they were making, what was her part in it?

The rain stopped. The ground was drier the further I got from the house, and the trees became clotted with birdsong. I was on the path that would take me to the street where we used to live, only a few short months ago; the street where Thew still lived now. I could go to his house and his mum would mother me whether I wanted mothering or not. But I needed to think. I turned off the path instead, and climbed up a steep little incline, partially hidden by trees. It came out at the edge of a mossy stone circle, in which an old oak tree stood with its roots radiating outwards. There was the shape of a woman in the trunk: a face that scowled and smiled, two breasts that protruded from the bark. She was an ancient but wounded tree: around the other side of her was a large hollow, almost as though the wood had been ripped open and scoured out. I crouched down and edged my way inside, giving any little creatures time to scuttle away. Once in, I sat with my knees pulled up to my chest, shivering and dripping rainwater.

If she was rehearsing, why couldn't she stop for a minute when I told her I needed her? I never asked her for anything, I never asked for a single thing.

I'm not your mother.

There was an empty feeling in my body. My body was an ugly sack of flesh around a void. I was nothing. Worthless. She didn't love me. She had never loved me.

But I'd thought she was going to change. When she'd found someone she loved and who loved her. Someone who thought she was "wonderful," who wanted her to be successful. She was the muse of a rich, talented artist, a man who wrote plays for her! Wasn't that enough? And there was money now. We used to go to the supermarket with a list, searching for the cheapest things. Now food appeared in the house; the fridge was always full, the pantry vast and stocked with every kind of thing you could imagine. Not that Mum ever ate any kind of thing. She lived on water and cigarettes, like a model or an actress. She thought food was disgusting.

Her not eating worried me, but when I'd hinted something about it, she'd sneered and said she was hardly going to take dietary advice from *me*. She was right; I was weak. I didn't have the strength to deny and starve, to flush out all my fat and be perfect. Be skin and bones. *Honeybones*, Tom called her. I pictured her bones all sweet and brittle like honeycomb. And him sucking on her bones, sucking the sweetness through his teeth.

Tom.

It was all about Tom. He was handsome, so tall and with such dark hypnotic eyes. I imagined his long white hand in the back of my hair and I felt shame rising in me, flushing my skin and making my breath stop in my throat. I knew what it meant. I knew what shame meant. Yes, even then: I saw what was spelled out for me – but only a part, not all. And it didn't matter what I glimpsed: I didn't know I had a choice. Everything that happened was inevitable; I was dragged along by the irresistible pull of love. I loved him. I loved my mother. But I loved *him* with a horrible plunging shame-filled love that scoured me out and left me sleepless. I *wanted* his hand in my hair, imagined it there, because maybe that would mean he loved me too. And he was mature: he wouldn't hate me for loving him. *Wanting* him. He was a man, not like other men. He always said he found other men disgusting, the way they treated women like they were things. He loved women. He *made love* to women. It wasn't the same as what other men did. I knew what other men did because their doings were everywhere. The things the boys at school said to me. The things they did. The sports teachers drooling over their magazine. The whistles and calls that tore through me, walking past a building site. A white van driving slowly by with the windows rolled down, and a man calling to me softly: *get in the van and I'll take you somewhere, I'll take you to see something nice.* They all saw what I was; my school uniform and hair in bunches just made it more obvious to them. But Tom didn't see me that way. He was my father, my teacher, my friend. He took me out of school to protect me from all that. The name-calling, the bullying, the graffiti, and the unanchored shame of it all. Because he loved me. And when my mother was terrible and untouchable, I would be *his* comfort and solace.

My rain-soaked clothes were cold now and I was shaking. I huddled in to myself and drifted in and out of sleep for a time. When I opened my eyes, the moss was glowing. There was the sound of something moving around the tree. Footsteps. I held my breath. Maybe not human, maybe a fox. But more likely to be Thew. A dark shadow fell across the moss and long legs appeared. Then the rest of him, squatting down to see inside the hollow.

"Thought you might be here," said Thew. He crawled into the hollow on his hands and knees, twisting around to get his arms and legs folded into the tiny space with me. Once he got his whole self inside the tree, I felt he was unfolding around me, that he was becoming part of the hollow. We sat in a tangle of legs, criss-crossed and pressed together. Just about able to see the shape of him, his outline blurring into the dark. But his voice was warm and clear.

"We barely fit in here anymore," he said.

I knew he wouldn't be able to see me either so I didn't bother to hide my face. I felt his eyes on me, anyway, searching me out. This was where we always came, since we were kids: to think, to talk and swap books and play games. But mostly to talk. And lately, we'd come here to kiss. The kissing had happened almost by accident, almost as if it were a continuation of talking. Sometimes it would happen halfway through a sentence. Moving our mouths, lips, tongues together to convey meaning; it almost felt like the same thing. We'd grown closer, kiss by kiss. But that all seemed a long time ago now.

"Are you okay?" he asked. And added, "I know you're not."

We didn't speak for a long time. It grew warmer, and calm in the hollow. I felt my legs melt into his legs, and stopped being able to tell which were which. There were hot patches where we were pressed together. I felt a knot of heat underneath me, unravelling. He was waiting for me to speak, and in the silence he was completely present. Like he was holding something open for me.

The words were in me but they wouldn't come up to the surface. There were so many things I couldn't tell him, couldn't even imagine telling him. At last I said, "I needed to think." My voice cracked on the word *needed*. Tears filled my throat. *I'm an idiot.*

His hands found mine in the darkness. There was warmth in them, strength, and something else I didn't understand, or didn't want to deal with. I pulled away and tucked my hands under my arms. This was all too much. His liking me was a terrible mistake, but he didn't seem to realise. When he finally saw me for what I was – I would see his feelings change. I knew I'd be able to feel it, feel everything he was feeling. Disgust. Pity. Contempt. I couldn't stand it. It would break my heart. Or maybe it wouldn't go that way. Maybe he already knew what I was, and this was just a game to him. He'd sweet talk me, act all nice so I'd let him fuck me, and then he'd go round telling his mates what a dirty slag I was. Like Tom said, *boys will be boys*. You're a fool to trust any of them.

"Do you not like me anymore?" His voice was soft and sounded nervous.

I shook my head. "It's not that."

"Okay. Good. Is it your mum? You can tell me."

I pictured her, mesmerised by herself in the mirror. Her hungry, sexy, thin body. Would it turn Thew on? He'd prefer her to me, anyway, obviously. I knew I couldn't explain what was wrong with her, or how she was hurting me. Because there wasn't anything wrong with her: she was perfect. And if her perfection hurt me then what did that mean? That I was jealous, inferior, and ugly. Thew would know I hated her and he'd think it was pathetic.

"Anna...where have you gone? Why won't you talk to me?"

"There's something wrong with me."

"What do you mean? No there isn't."

"There is. I think I'm really crazy, properly. I don't what I am, I'm broken. I don't even feel like a real person anymore."

Tears came from nowhere and I couldn't stop them. *I'm not a real person.* It sounded such a strange thing to say but it hurt so much. This time I didn't push Thew away when his hands reached for mine. I cried helplessly and Thew said, over and over, "You're not broken. You're real. It's okay."

But he didn't know about the other girls, the endless girls, the Dreemy Peeple. He didn't know about the mirror mothers or the shark-headed woman who swam the hallways. He didn't know about the voices that possessed me at night, or about how I could feel fingers pushing between my legs, pulling on my breasts, how I couldn't wake up from it. He didn't know (did he?) about the graffiti in the girls' toilets, or the way the sports teachers had laughed at me, like I was the same to them as the girls in their magazine. He didn't know that some of the boys at school whispered "slag" as they passed and tried to grab me between the legs. He didn't know why Tom had taken me out of school, only that he had, and that I was never going back. I kept it all from him and hoped he didn't know what everyone else knew: that I was nothing. That I didn't matter. And now I was crying all over him, so pathetic. He must hate me.

I pulled away, sniffing back tears. "I'm sorry," I said.

"You don't have to say sorry."

"I do. You don't understand. We live in different worlds now. You don't know how it is for me anymore. Everything's different. Even time. Even time is different now."

"Of course it's different. Death changes things. The grief makes you feel broken. I know that's how it was when my dad died, anyway. You said it yourself: you've fallen out of time."

"It's not that," I said. But something was bothering me. I ran over his words in my mind, trying to understand.

"Look. Why don't you stay at mine for a bit? Mum's got the spare room all done out for you. She misses you, you know."

I didn't respond. I thought of Thew's mum, who always said, *call me Lita,* but I never did because I wasn't brave enough. She'd cook chicken and rice and peas on a Sunday and say, *you need to learn to cook this for Thew,* and Thew would say, *Mum, you're embarrassing me* and I'd say, *he can cook his own dinner.* She would have put a flannelette cover on the bed in the spare room. I could picture it. I'd stayed there so many times it was like my own house. But I'd barely been there since Tom had taken me out of school. I didn't walk home with Thew anymore. And besides, I couldn't cope with too much normality.

"Please," Thew said. "I don't like thinking about the two of you in that big house. Sometimes I dream about that house. It gives me nightmares." He paused. "About the cully king."

The cully king. The sound of the words filled the air with beating wings. I could feel Thew's dreaming, the quality of his fear. I thought of when he had been a fox, huge and quick and red on the stair. I saw him flesh out and sink into the muscle of his dream. Was it a dream? Did it happen?

"The dreams make me feel sick. Like a flower of sickness opening up inside me."

It was a strange way to express it, but I understood. I felt it too.

"At the funeral..." he started.

"No," I said. "I don't want to talk about that."

"Okay."

"What about the funeral? No, I don't want to know."

We were silent again. I was thinking now, thinking hard. There was something I needed to understand. Something...a secret I was holding, a key to turn the world. It was in something Thew had said, but I couldn't think what, it eluded me like a golden fish darting through my hands.

"Okay, tell me," I said. But then, "Wait."

Sunlight crept into the hollow and glinted in the soil and leaves. I dug for something with my fingers and found metal. I held it up to Thew.

"I can't see what it is," he said.

"A key," I said.

It dissolved on my skin. There was nothing where the key had been, only my fingers, pressed uselessly together.

"The key is to remember," said Thew.

Something was unravelling inside my mind. Ever since the funeral, things had been so strange. And then after the funeral, we had all come home. All come home to the house of mirrors. And everything was so strange.

There was the funeral. The funeral...it had rained so hard. Our shoes sank into the mud. And after the funeral, we came back home to the house of mirrors. The three of us. Our family. Anna, and Sarah, and Tom.

After the funeral. We all came home.

All of us. Mum, and Tom, and me.

After the funeral.
We'd all come home.
All of us.
Even the one who was dead.

⁂

Up stairs, down stairs, along the winding corridor, onto the landing and to my mother's door. Raining, raining, trailing mud and water from hair and clothes. Conscious of my body moving in a dislocated way. No thought in my mind.

I hammered on the door, making rainwater fly from my fists, and I screamed come out, come out – but my words were incoherent, even to me. I was screaming, a wordless mutilated scream.

She opened the door.

My mother. A bone mother. Face thin and white as a blister of milk, dark puddles for eyes. Her hair a writhing mess. Her lips a bloody stain.

She'd done this to me. No. I'd done this to myself. Somehow I'd done it. There was a huge black lake at the centre of myself, a drowning lake with grabbing seaweed tentacles, an inky well into which parts of my life tumbled and sank below the surface, to be devoured. I had forgotten myself. I had done things to myself. I knew, I had known…but I'd lied and deceived and covered it all up. But no, no, she'd done this, she'd betrayed me. Us. What had she done, what had she become?

She was staring through me, as though I wasn't really there.

"You're not my mother," I said through sobs of air. "You're dead, Mum. You're dead."

She slapped me hard across my face. The slap stunned me, knocked all the words out of my mouth. There was a spray of rain across the wallpaper.

"*How dare you*?" Her voice was terrible. Broken, slurring like one of the Dreemy Peeple I'd thrown out the window.

My skin was burning in the shape of her hand. She was lying. She was dead and she was too proud or too ashamed to admit it. She was dead but she still wouldn't stop. She wouldn't give up.

"*You're* dead," she said. "You, Anna Carrow. You're dead! Dead dead dead and it's disgusting."

"Stop," I said. "Stop being so fucking pathetic."

"I'm in *love*," she hissed. "He loves me and you're a jealous dead bitch."

I'm not dead. I was there, at your funeral. Everyone's shoes were ruined. Soaked from coat to bone. The gravestones sinking into mud. All the starlings, all the crows, gathered at the edges, ready to pick over the leavings. I couldn't remember the priest or the service and only once I think I found myself with Thew holding my hand between his, the stained glass glowing dully around us. But then he was gone and it was the graveyard and the birds and we were burying *you*, Mum.

"You," I said.

She was standing there, her bone hands clenched into white fists, gazing at me in defiance of everything I'd said.

I jumped at a soft step behind me. My mother's black puddled eyes went wide and still. Long white fingers that smelled of vanilla settled over my shoulders.

"Hello," said Tom. "What's all this?"

"*Don't tell him*." Mum slithered back inside the bedroom and slammed the door in my face.

%

"Anna! You're wet through. Come and sit by the fire."

He led me through the house, through doors I'd never seen before, along a wide gallery that looked down on a ballroom, with polished wooden floors. We had a ballroom? I wondered to myself. He was moving quickly and I was running to catch up. I couldn't understand why I was so cold and wet, then I remembered. We'd been to a funeral.

"What were you doing? Why were you disturbing your mother?"

He didn't wait for an answer and I was glad, because I didn't have one. I couldn't remember now. I remembered the graveyard, and falling in the mud. But there was something else I'd forgotten.

We weren't alone in the house. There were others present. They watched from silent hidden places. And there was music in the air. In the house. A faint lilting music, like a nursery rhyme. One I couldn't quite remember. It was in the house, it was in the things of the house. A thousand threads of music woven into the walls and the books and the chairs and everything else. A thousand thousand strands of music weaving the world. Why hadn't I heard it before? But I had heard it. It was always there, under everything. I'd heard it but I hadn't been conscious.

In Tom's library, the music was louder. Objects were heavy with it. I touched the top of a table and heard a ripple run through the notes.

"Don't touch," said Tom. "Stand by the fire."

The soles of my shoes grew warm, my T-shirt and jeans started steaming as rain evaporated in the heat. Tom came up behind me; he picked up the length of my hair and patted it between the folds of a towel. I froze. His breath was at my ear. His breath was on my neck.

It was too late to say no.

The music grew louder. Clamouring inside my head until I couldn't hear anything else. I took a step away from the fire, but he held me there, hands gripping my shoulders.

"You shouldn't go into the garden, Anna. You shouldn't leave the house. The garden is infested with horrible things. All sorts of nasty little creatures that burrow under your skin and eat their way through your veins to your brains."

I'd stopped breathing. His hands moved slowly down my arms, brushing my skin with the tips of his fingers. My clothes were scalding me but I dared not move. I couldn't remember why I'd come here. So hard to think straight, with that music playing, and the warmth in the room and the scalding pain of my clothes... A fierce exhaustion pulled at me. Why had I gone into the garden, in all that rain...what a strange thing to do, what a *stupid little bitch*...now the fire felt so hypnotic, so alive, weaving itself into the music...hot enough to melt my bones to honey...

"Maybe it already happened," said Tom. His voice was at my ear, close enough that I felt his lips move against my skin. Cold, flickering mouth. "The doctors think something like that may be happening to your mother. An infestation. Some kind of beetle or worm."

No, no, that wasn't possible. She was not infested, only I was. She hadn't been in the garden; only I had been in the garden. I could tell I was infested with something: they were all over me, burrowing, crawling under my skin.

Tom pulled away from me. I backed away from the fire, and stumbled into Tom's desk chair. I span the chair around and saw a notebook, open in front of me. *She fights against nothing, you watch her every night. Her legs spread wide apart and you try to grab her there, and she loves it, she wants it. She's smiling. You can force your hands inside her and it will be wet and slick and she'll make those noises they all make. She fights you off but you know better than her. She wants it, they all want it, they're all the same. Full of dirt on the inside. Panting and mewling like animals.* I looked over at Tom. He wrote this? I felt sick, a flower of sickness opening inside me. My thoughts came to a dizzying halt; Tom's hands snatched the notebook away from me.

"I told you no looking," he said.

"You said no touching," I replied.

Annoyance flashed over his face; then he laughed. "Clever girl."

"Did you write that?"

I turned to the notebook. It was gone. And now I saw there was someone else with Tom. There was someone else, covering Tom's back, overlapping him. I saw it quite plainly. The other had dense black feathers, a beak, claws. It was as though Tom were two entities, or more, or not a person at all. Shifting between man and bird. *Possessed.*

He leaned back on the desk. His arms were crossed, wings folded. "Did I ever tell you about my first wife, Rose?"

Rose. I pictured a woman in water. A face like the head of a shark, ugly, a monstrous mouth locked and secured in a metal cage. Even her name made me flinch.

"You remind me of Rose, you do. She was a writer, or tried to be. But she ended up mad. Insane. She saw things that weren't there, had these terrible hallucinations. I nursed her, you know, right up until the end. They wanted me to put her away, but I'd never do that. I wanted to care for her myself. It wasn't easy, Anna. It was terrible sometimes. Sometimes she saw me and she'd fly into a terrible rage, try to claw out my eyes. I treated that woman like a queen, I sacrificed years to her, and that's how she repaid me."

He sighed, and stood up straight. "Why are women such bitches?"

I flinched. He wanted me to answer him. I didn't know what to say.

"Oh dear, you must think I sound like a sexist pig. But what I mean is – what I mean, Anna, is I've seen it all before. The hallucinations, the sleepwalking, the dreaming with your eyes open. Seeing things, hearing things – it's exactly how it was with Rose. Exactly the same. And knowing now what I wish I'd known back then – I think you should see someone. Let's go back to Doctor Lumna. Or someone who understands how to treat a severe psychosis like this."

Severe psychosis? I was crazy, I was mad like Rose? For a moment I was indignant but then I realised: no – it made sense. Yes, it explained everything. I was crazy. I was crazy and none of this was real. It was all in my head. Dreams, hallucination, madness...*schizophrenia, psychosis, delusion.* Thank god, it was all in my head. I chanted the words like they were charms. *Schizophrenia, psychosis, delusion.* They were diseases and diseases could be treated. I could be fixed. There were drugs for people like me, there were treatments that worked. Tom had money, so I would get the best care and everything was going to be fine. I would go back to Doctor Lumna and there would be a drug that would fix me. Or there was always the hospital. But the thought of the hospital made me afraid.

"Maybe I shouldn't have taken you out of school. Maybe that legitimised your perceptions. Your delusions about what was happening to you there. See, where Rose went wrong is she was never able to admit to it. She never gave in. She maintained that she was sane, right up until the end. That was the extent of her madness, she genuinely believed it was true. Did you hear, what she did to herself in the end? It was...it was very upsetting."

What had she done to herself? She'd done it to herself? The cage – or what did he mean? It was awful, what she'd done, whatever it was. Oh god... But I was better than Rose. I accepted it. I understood. None of it was real. And yet accepting my condition did not loosen any of its power over me. Even now, I was hallucinating. I saw that Tom's lips were moving, but heard another voice speaking, a voice whispering in between Tom's words. A coarse and ancient whisper. Dust and feathers caught in the back of the throat. My skin crawled.

...and i'll melt your bones and scrape them out of your body, i'll sew your mouth shut with barbed wire, and sew your hands together,

finger to finger…i'll scour out your skull and stuff it with feathers… you won't be able to move or speak or think…you won't be able to say a word against me and I'll tell everyone you begged me to do it to you, you loved it, you got on your hands and knees and let me

"I think an episode of hospitalisation might be recommended. I know that sounds scary. It's a very difficult kind of madness, when a person confuses reality with a dream. They diagnosed Rose with all sorts of things but she wouldn't have any of it. We could have helped her so much. And your mother…"

My mother…

i'll ruin your language and leave you no words of your own. nothing belongs to you except emptiness. i'll give you broken glass to chew on. tie your hair to the bedposts, smash your feet so you can't run away and tell everyone how you made me do it to you, little schoolgirl slut made it so i couldn't help myself

They were both talking at once, both entities, in their very different voices. The bird's voice was saturated in hatred. The bird overlapped Tom, flickering around him like a shadowy aura. I felt sickness flower in me and petal outwards. This was the madness Tom was talking about. It was happening now, here in this room, and I had to tell him. I had to let him help me. I didn't want to be like Rose, so stubborn and ugly. I couldn't imagine anything worse, than to be that way when you had a choice. Tom was my stepfather and I should trust him; I could trust him completely.

"It's happening now," I said. "I'm hearing things. Seeing things. Right now."

"Tell me." He was at my side in an instant. His hands were on mine. I felt talons pressing into my skin.

"There's two of you," I said. "You and...something. A bird thing."

a bird king you dirty bitch get it right

"Oh fucking hell," said Tom.

He reached up his right hand and snapped his fingers in the air. I felt a little jolt go through me. A second of blankness and then revival. Tom's face wore an expression of confusion that quickly morphed into anger. His eyes boiled green and glossy black and he held up both his hands as though examining his palms.

It was his hands. There was something wrong with his hands.

A voice climbed up on my shoulder and whispered horribly into my ear: *oh, but those are not my hands.*

The front door slammed and the house shook and the day started all over again.

%

The three of us side by side in the mirror. His long white hand in the back of my hair. His fingers pressing into my scalp. My mother on the other side of me in her long clingy black slip. Her shoulders like two bony wings. I hated my dress, the black satin. Puffed sleeves and petticoats. A child's party dress, only it's a funeral we're going to, not a party. Next to Tom and Mum, I looked like a child. A big fat overgrown child. Mum was all thin bones like a model. Tom looked sleek in his cashmere suit, so fine and black it was almost not there at all.

"Ready, my love?"

Through the mirrors, into the house inside the house. Up and up, and round, and down, and over and over, stepping through one house to the other and back again in a thousand reiterations of a footstep. It was to be mine, all of this. I was promised. The house inside the house opened up to us like walls melting away. *I'll give you as many houses as you want,* he said. We ran past the ballroom, up a spiralling turret, along twisting turning corridors that led to a kitchen with a huge empty hearth. Through the open back door there was the garden, drenched in rain, a blur of green and black.

"We won't bury you in the garden," he said. "It'll only make you dream and we've all had enough of that."

We ran backwards and inside-out through the house to the cellar door. The hallways unfolded and refolded around us. The cellar door pulsed in its frame like a beast in a cage. I'd never been down to the cellar before. I don't think I'd even known it was there. But of course this house would have a cellar, many cellars, many cellars all connected by passages: by visions and transitions; by steps you didn't realise you were taking. We went down, deeper and deeper still. The walls were mossy and weeping water. They glittered with sticky trails, orange slugs and tiny white egg-like flowers. We splashed through puddles towards a faint grey blur of light and came out into a field of rain. Rain beating the earth into water. Gravestones, sinking into mud. A small group of people standing under black umbrellas. Their ankles were sinking through the grass, they were picking their feet up and trying to find firm ground. I was among them, under the black umbrellas. The rain drowned out the priest's voice to a solemn drone, and Tom's white hand in my hair confused me. *We're standing side by side in the mirror in our strange black clothes.* They're lowering the coffin into a grave full of rain. It sank quickly, and bubbles rose in the black water. Across from me, standing over the grave, a dark shape grew visible under the grey torrent. The shape moved towards me. A woman's form but her head was mutilated and irregular. The shape of the cage around her thick-skinned, ugly, hungry face.

I screamed myself awake. I was sleepwalking, lost in the house inside the house.

No dreaming in the house of mirrors.

I was in the hallway, watching the endless girls. I was just like them. In my flouncy black dress with the puffed sleeves and my hair so curly and lips so pink and fat and smooth and shiny. My skin so smooth and numb. And the blood on my face, the rainwater and the blood. All in my head.

My mother was behind me on the staircase, making a noise like crashing wings. I watched her in the mirror as she moved stiffly up the stairs. Her body moving out of time. We had fallen out of time.

Then Tom was there.

"Anna! You're wet through. Come and sit by my fire."

He took my hand and led me through the house, up stairs and down stairs, through doors I'd never seen before, along a wide gallery that looked down on a ballroom, with polished wooden floors.

"Wait. Wait!"

"No time!" Tom cried. "We better get you nice and dry and toasty."

We were running now, faster and faster, yet we didn't

seem to be moving at all. We were in a house of music and it played one long doomy note. My heart thudded in my chest, I couldn't catch my breath and then – we were in the library. The fire roared and licked out at me.

"Wait," I said. "We've been here before."

"Don't touch," said Tom. "Stand by the fire."

I wasn't touching anything. But I recognised his words. As though it had all unfolded exactly this way before. As though there was a script, and I was playing my part. What was my next line? He was behind me, patting my hair between the folds of a towel.

I froze. It felt too late to say no.

My voice was tiny when I spoke. "You're scaring me."

He stopped drying my hair, let the towel drop onto the hearth. "Silly girl! What's to be afraid of?"

I shook my head. I couldn't say anything more; that had taken all my courage and I was shaking now. Tom looked at me carefully, and I felt he was appraising me. Summing me up to himself. Then suddenly I realised his expression was one of pain, and I felt horribly sad for hurting him. I hadn't meant to.

"Oh, Anna. It's just...I'm so lonely."

He staggered back to his seat and crumpled into it. All the youth and strength seemed to leave his body and he hung his head in his hands. I went to him and knelt on the floor at his feet. He took my hands in his; they were cold and bony and I could hardly feel them at all. My own hands felt rubbery and numb.

"You've seen your mother," he said. "She's not been a wife to me in a long time, Anna."

I understood. He needed to be loved, too. And my mother, so cold and – so dead. ("Don't tell him," she'd said. Should I tell him?) I stroked his hands with my own, numb hands. My skin looked weirdly smooth and plasticky in the firelight.

"I shouldn't be telling you any of this," he said. "It's not your problem. Why should you care? Someone as wonderful as you." He sniffed. He shifted in the seat. I could see the hard bulge at his crotch; he squeezed my hands and gently moved them towards it.

It was too late to say no.

He lightly pushed my hand against his crotch and moved it ever so slightly so I could feel the hard lump under my rubbery palm. No, it must have been an accident, because he was still sat with his head hung, and an expression of pure sorrow on his face.

I pulled my hand away and got to my feet.

"Anna..." It was a groan. He grabbed my hand and looked up at me. "You're so different to your mother. So warm and full of life. In some ways I think I married her to get closer to you. I'm very drawn to you, Anna. Do you understand?"

No. I didn't understand, not fully. Was he saying he loved me? Was this love?

He put his head in his hands. I didn't know what to say to him. I didn't want to make him so sad. If he *wanted* me, then what could I do about it? It wasn't something I felt I had to decide. It was more like an inevitable outcome of who we were, of this situation. I could initiate it: that might make me feel braver. But I knew that the decision was already made, and I was not an agent in that decision, but the object that had been decided upon.

I found I was in front of a book shelf, running my fingers along the covers. I felt the ridges of leather and board through fingers that felt thick and far away. Tom held his head in his hands. It must be awful for him, I thought. I'm glad that he loves me. I felt swollen inside, full of pride and terror. I tried to make out the book titles, but the letters were too faded and the light too dim and I wasn't really thinking. I picked a book at random, a thick leather-bound volume. Incongruously, it weighed hardly anything. It smelled of fake vanilla. I opened the cover. The pages were blank. Ancient, thin, stained paper. But no words or marks of any kind.

I made some kind of noise and Tom looked up. He looked furious. I dropped the empty book on the floor, pulled out the next book, and the next. They were the same. All blank. Tom sprang to my side and grabbed my wrists.

"Stop it," he said.

I thought that was it; that he would push me down then onto the floor. But he let go of my wrists and picked up one of the books.

"That bitch," he said.

At his desk, he flipped through a pile of papers, notebooks, letters. He held them up to me and then threw them to the floor. All blank. There was nothing on any of them. All the words had leached out of the room.

"It's her," he said to me. "Rose. Do you understand?"

There was something in the bin next to Tom's desk. I pulled it out from the screwed-up pieces of blank paper, facsimiles of so many abandoned attempts.

This House of Mirrors
Rose Liddell

> *Anna you are dreeming. Come into the under-the-house. This house of mirrors is not your home. Let's go dancing all night long. The cully king is raging mad. Come into the under-the-house. The thing the king I love to sing and*

The words were fading away as I read them. *You are dreeming. Come into the under-the-house.* The words sang in my mind like a nursery rhyme: come into the under-the-house. The under-the-house. Why did they want me to go there? Tom snatched the book from me; it was all emptied out now.

Why would she unwrite her own book?

"She's crazy," Tom said. "Do you see now, what we've all been up against? She won't let anyone have a single shred of happiness! I thought she was dead and gone but she keeps! Coming! Back!" He threw objects at the wall to punctuate his fury. Now he came to me and took my hands. His eyes were wild and blazed through me.

"She hates you, Anna. She hates anyone I love. She'll hunt you down and torment you. It's already happening, isn't it? You can tell me, Anna. I've seen it all before. She's got to you, hasn't she?"

He didn't wait for an answer before continuing. "She's possessed you. She's taken over your mind and that's why you're mad. She was psychotic and – to be honest – a fucking bitch when she was alive. But in death she's worse. Look what she's done to you! And your mother! Look what she's done to *me*."

He cast his hands around to suggest the devastation in the library. All the blank, emptied out books.

"You should leave me, Anna. She'll never give up. She'll never let us be happy. Go, leave me. You don't want a horrible old man like me, anyway. You're young and so wonderful. You'll have a good life without me."

He sat back on the chair, head in his hands again. His shoulders shook as though he were sobbing. Or laughing. No, he was crying...I saw his eyes through his fingers. Pooled in sadness and despair. I felt my heart would break for him. That was love, wasn't it? But it wasn't easy, love. There were all the things you had to do for it. I felt Tom's pain, and his need; I felt his emotions like they were my own. And I wanted so much to make it all okay again. So much. I would have done anything.

It struck me that Tom didn't even know the worst of it: that Rose had killed my mother. I couldn't bring myself to tell him, to betray her, not yet. Instead I concentrated on my hatred for Rose. It was pure and brilliant. I intended to destroy her. I didn't know how, but I knew it was my task, to destroy her and set Tom free. An exorcism. A purging of evil from the house. Tom would love me more than he loved anyone. And I would be free again, to sleep, to dream. To move through time in an ordinary way.

Anna, you are dreeming.

Come into the under-the-house.

Tom was watching me through his fingers.

"What are you going to do, Anna?"

I was going to destroy Rose, once and for all.

"I'll help you," I said. "I'm here for you."

He smiled. All the sadness left him in an instant and he beamed at me like he was the happiest man alive. But even then, something flickered about his shoulders and his hair. Something cruel and feathered. Something with a voice like dirt.

%

I was watching the girls in the mirror. My black dress felt too tight; the puffed sleeves were digging into the flesh of my arms, leaving itchy weals of red and white. The full petticoat skirt was rough and unwieldy. But how pretty they were, these endless mirror girls. Was it the glitter of moonlight sparkling on the glass? Or was it a round cheek, a dark eye, a full lip...they were bloodied, jangled girls. Bruises on their necks and blood on their collars. Pretty, pretty. Falling into the silver rooms of reflection. A kind of victory, wasn't it? Now I was pretty at last, now I lived in the thin air of beauty, under its trembling veneer. Losing my fat, ugly, terrible body – I could already feel it loosening, the flesh becoming something else. Look at the pretty girls. Watch their pretty eyes, calling me deeper into the mirror.

Something moved on the stair behind me, but the mirror reflected nothing. I listened to the swish of watery skirts dragging over the floors. The clank, the rattle, and the guttural whispered groans. It was her. It was Rose.

Rose. Ruining everything. Making everything seem wrong and mad.

I knew it was *her* in the library, emptying out the books, haunting Tom with feathers. Making me dream terrible things. Tom would never hurt me. If he loved me, it wasn't like *that.* It was something pure, something that only the two of us could understand. Because of Rose, it was all tainted. I was frightened I would hurt him with my delusions. I didn't want to be a stupid girl crying *rape* because a man *wanted* me. Or I thought he did, for a brief moment, while a ghost pushed her horrible hands into my brain. If I told anyone that he'd touched me…but he hadn't, had he? It was me who had touched him.

Rose. She had got to me. She was in my mind, twisting my thoughts. Whispering terrible secrets in my ear. Turning love into a dirty, frightening thing.

I hated her. But I wasn't afraid. Rose was nothing to me. I would make *her* afraid and send her away forever. I'd let her know that Tom didn't love her, that he deserved to move on and love again. I didn't think about how I'd do it. I knew that when the time came I would be moved by the force of love that had powerfully arisen in me. I felt invincible. Because Tom loved me. He loved me. I was loved. *Me.* Fat little Anna who everyone said was a worthless slag. Loved by a handsome rich older artist. My lover? Maybe I could call him that. Soon.

All I had to do was this one little thing.

The girls in the mirror slipped away, round corners and out of sight. But I remained. And Rose moved behind me, reflecting nothing but a grey shimmer in the glass.

I stalked her through the house. But the house wouldn't stay still, and I found it increasingly difficult to move through air which was dense like swollen clouds of black rain. I felt I couldn't see – but it was all clear before me. The landings, with their various carpets and furniture. Up and down stairs. Everything solid and visible and real. So real. But I felt nothing was there; I felt I was navigating a dark cloud and here and there I felt myself submerged in it, in water that was solid blackness. I could breathe; but I felt I could not breathe. I was on the landing outside my mother's room. I was nowhere at all.

The front door slammed – and the air cracked in a jagged line. A bolt of thunder shattered everything in the house to pieces, and wild white light streamed through the cracks. A glimpse of a broken, beautiful world.

I suddenly knew I was drowning, and these were all the drowning thoughts that flooded my mind. I was dying and I was a fool to fight it, because it didn't matter, and it was better to die. Still I flailed madly and tried to rise, tried to move limbs that felt highly attenuated. Not really mine at all. I was a pair of numb hands fluttering. I choked on air and rainwater rushed inside me. I was standing in cold water up to my shoulders. In a pitch black, soundless space.

She was there, in that space with me. I had no doubt. A shock went through me, and I was afraid, but it wasn't Rose that scared me. It was the thought that she might disappear, and leave me here alone. She was terrible. But when I thought of what she had done to herself, I could imagine, could see myself, doing it. Nailing my own tongue down so I couldn't speak. Couldn't tell lies and hurt other people. I wanted to be made to stop.

Anna, you are dreeming.

Dreeming, was I? Dreeming. Yes. I ran backwards through the mirrors. My body was everywhere, broken and repeated. Every movement multiplied a thousand times. I was nowhere but I was in every reflection, a girl shattering out into distant dark. I fell, we all fell; I staggered, we all staggered; we were all disoriented and sick. Running backwards through the house of mirrors. A long doomy note reverberated through everything; it was thunder, and inside the mirrors it was raining, always raining. It was thunder, it was the slam of the front door. It was a snap of his fingers and the day starting all over again.

I had always been lost. The day of the funeral had started at the end.

I had to work back to the beginning.

We were standing side by side in the mirror. His long white hand in the back of my hair.

I am dreeming.

The key is to remember.

"We're just about to begin," he said.

%

The church was lit inside by candles and whatever rained-out gloomlight could penetrate the old and dirty stained-glass windows. Tom touched my elbow to guide me and I stumbled. He grabbed me, stopped me from falling. I noticed there was rainwater on the stone floor of the church. It seemed to have been raining forever. I noticed the pews weren't straight, but in haphazard rows. At first I thought no one had come, but then I saw there were people sitting in some of the pews. I thought I saw Thew but when I turned to look again it wasn't him. There was a Dreemy Peeple doll where he'd been sitting. Its plastic legs sticking out towards the stage.

I looked at Tom but he was looking ahead, at the coffin that was raised up on the platform. He touched me again, guiding me to my seat. I twisted around. There were Dreemy Peeple in other pews too. They were broken: some of them were missing limbs, their faces were cracked, and they were muddy.

threw my toys out of the pram, you nasty little psycho

He was there. The cully king was there.

I turned to Tom.

"Are you okay, love?"

"I can see them again. And that voice came back. That horrible bird...thing."

He stroked my arm and smiled sympathetically. "Remember your breathing exercises. Nice deep breaths and remember darling it's all in your head. And you've been feeling much better, haven't you? This...thing, with your mum, it's given you a little blip."

A little blip. I breathed deeply and counted to ten. He was right, I could see things clearly now, as they really were. There was Thew and his mum. She gave a little wave and smile. Thew frowned, asking a question with his face. *What's going on?* I shrugged. What was he even asking? Tom touched my shoulder to get me to turn around. He didn't like Thew much. He said he was a typical boy; he knew his type. The type who pretended to be all nice and sweet, but really they're out for one thing. Why else would a boy like that be interested in a girl like you? Why would a popular boy be friends with you when everyone else at school turned against you? Be suspicious, he warned me. Tom was frank with me; he wanted me to be able to protect myself. Boys like that think girls like you are only worth a fuck. But Tom was an artist. He didn't think the way other men thought.

Rain splashed onto the top of the coffin and I thought, that's strange. Why don't they fix the roof?

Now the vicar was there, walking over the platform, and all around me, crows and starlings wriggled through holes in the stone walls of the church, greasy feathered bodies worming in. Some gathered at the edges of the platform. One perched upon the Vicar's podium. He didn't seem to notice. He lifted his head to begin the service and I saw he would not be able to. Something had happened to him; he had been violated, obliterated from his own body. The cully king unfolded himself and stepped down from the podium. He swept his hands about, indicating the platform was now his stage.

time to tango!

I knew he was the cully king because he couldn't be anything else. His wings were slick and greasy, his beak shone cruelly in the gloom. And when he spoke, his voice made me feel like I was choking on feathers and dust, and it made me feel ugly to hear it. It made me want to crawl out of my skin.

I looked wildly around for Tom. He had his head down and his hands clasped together so tightly he was quivering. I realised the service had started. But for me: my brain was putting on a special performance. Only Tom understood. But I couldn't speak to him now, and ruin the service. He was in deep mourning and I needed to be there for him, not make things harder. I had to endure it, that was all. Remember it's not real. It's all in your head. I breathed deeply and counted to ten. But all the while I counted silently in my head, the cully king was opening the coffin and pulling my mother to her feet in odd, emaciated jolts. Her long and slinky black dress had mud on the hem. My bone mother.

She's practising for her part. She's really wonderful.

She slipped from his grasp, crumpled down and flung her arms around his legs. He reached down and grabbed her hair in his fist. Lifted her quickly to her feet, like pulling a rabbit from a hat. She dangled for a moment, skinny and wretched, her legs streaked in mud or blood or both. A spotlight fell on her, casting her shadow behind, black velvet shadow, quivering at the edges. And her face! oh so beautiful, a perfect victim. Spilling tears that glistened in the hollow light. It was all a game, a play, a masque my mind was inventing. But there was something horribly real in the way the cully king was holding her up by her hair.

what a nasty scrawny looking thing. well, she will do for the purposes of demonstration…

The Dreemy Peeple behind me made sounds through their plastic speakers. Crying or laughing, I couldn't tell. Stuttering mechanical outbursts.

behold…

The cully king took a large pair of silver sewing scissors from under his wing. He held them in one hand, and Mum's hair in the other, wrapped tightly round his fist. Now he sounded bored when he spoke, and recited his lines dully.

o look, it is the queen of knives!

what a sight for happy eyes
she looks like something the cat's dragged in…
well, let this fucking show begin

The cully king smiled nastily, his mouth full of nails. He looked right at me. I tried to shrink down into my seat, to disappear. He winked slowly, and in a voice I thought no one else could hear, said,

so sorry for your loss!

He opened the scissors and snapped them in the air two times, *snick snack!*, and then, with the third flashing-bright scissoring, he cut my mother away from her hair. She fell, folded up like a marionette. The cully king rolled the long wet hair into an untidy ball, and stuffed it under his wing. Regarding her impatiently, tapping his foot on the water-softened wood, he said,

stand up! up, up, up on your feet, you pathetic bitch. let's get on with it!

Mum staggered to her feet. A sickening struggle. She could barely hold herself up. She raised a hand to her head, terrified, bewildered. Her beautiful hair. And cast her eyes around the room, looking for something, beseeching someone… She didn't see me, pinned there in dark shadows. But then she never saw me. She never had. She never knew I was there.

The cully king giggled, and quickly resumed his bored demeanour.

that is the first wound, and the gentlest cut
the second one will stop you being such a lying slut

Laughter behind me. Or was it howls of despair? Mechanical howls from the plastic insides of the Dreemy Peeple. On the stage, Mum looked around wildly. Her eyes wide with fear and desperation. She shook her head, no, no. I wanted to scream, to yell something, to make it stop. Tom would make it stop. But I couldn't look away. And the cully king moved without mercy. He grabbed Mum's face, grappled with her head, put his black-gloved hand into her mouth. She was choking, softly flailing with her arms. I closed my eyes. There were three sharp snips and then a rush, a pouring onto the wood. When I opened my eyes, the cully king was holding my mother's tongue aloft in his fist.

I was not alive. Not awake. I was sleepwalking. It was all in my head.

But it felt so real.

The cully king laughed and gave the tongue a bloody kiss before tucking it under his wing.

a whore who cannot speak, cannot lie

as for the third injunction, let us try

He knelt at my mother's feet and drew a hammer from under his wing. His mouth filled with nails. He nailed her tattered satin shoes to the wood. Each strike of the hammer reverberated through my bones. And Mum's strangulated, tongueless cries. And the rain coming in. And the splashes of blood that fell like rain. A crow hopped nearby, greedily pecking, and the cully king tried to pulverise it with his hammer, catching several of its wing feathers under the iron. It made a broken, flapping escape.

The cully king wiped the bloody silver scissorblades against his filthy wings. He knelt behind Mum. Grinned. Winked. He folded his wings in imitation of the vicar.

now what can we say about this woman? well to be honest she was kind of a bitch

not to speak ill of the dead

and by the way i want you to know this is all fully consensual

The cully king scooped up my mother's shadow from where it rested on the floor. He lifted it in his arms like a child, so fine and black it was almost not there at all. Mum was grunting, trying to say something, and every time she did, it made the cully king stop and giggle. I heard each one of her tongueless sounds as words inside my mind. *No. Please. I'm sorry.*

oh please. you asked for this part. you begged for it.

Where the shadow met the flesh, he cut. He ripped it away in his fists, his foot on her back as he tore it up from its roots deep in flesh and bone.

She clutched her face, blood and tears and rain pouring through her fingers. The cully king gathered up her limp black shadow in his arms, crushed it into a ragged bundle, and shoved it under his wing. He declaimed, in a bored and mocking voice:

that was her soul i took to my desire

and let it be a warning to every little liar

The Dreemy Peeple made tinny broken noises, half-words and stutters coming from the speakers under their dresses. The cully king looked at them with seething contempt.

who writes this shit, anyway

He left the platform with an angry flourish of his wings, and the vicar slid from the podium, and fell sprawled on the little wooden steps.

My mother stood there still, her shoes nailed to the wood, her hair shorn and her tongue a bleeding stump, and her shadow ripped out at the quick. There was rain falling into her open coffin. Rain dripped through the roof, mingling with the blood at her feet.

She smiled then, horribly. And took a bow.

%

Then Thew was pressing my hand between his hands and saying my name. "Anna…Anna…Anna…" Like a heartbeat.

I smiled at him but my smile felt crooked and crazy. I was looking around for my mum, I knew she was there somewhere. The coffin had gone already, gone on ahead to the grave. I didn't know where Tom was now – no I did, he was there, he was in the lobby, shaking hands with someone. He glanced at me and frowned, and I thought, what's wrong? There's something wrong with my hair, my face.

Thew squeezed my hand and spoke with urgency. "Anna, what's happening? I know something's happening and I want to help."

come into the under-the-house

They were here. My dreeming sisters.

"I've fallen out of time," I said.

"Is it him?" Thew lowered his voice still further. "Is it *the cully king*?"

The cully king. The cully king. Did Thew really say *the cully king*? Or was I making shapes from his sounds, was I making it all up in my head? How did he know about the cully king, then? Could he see him too? Could he see the Dreemy Peeple?

it's a dreemy world for dreemy people

"How do you know," I asked.

"I know," said Thew.

come into the under-the-house

"I'll come now," I said.

And I was already there.

⁂

And I was already there. In darkness. Lying on my back under tightly-made covers. I didn't think I could move; my body was stiff and disconnected. I managed to wriggle the covers loose, and thrashed around to free myself, senseless limbs flailing and flopping.

Finally I sat up. I sensed a vast expanse of cold space around me. There was a smell in the room, of bleach and instant coffee (an eruption of laughter, a roar of wet soft mouths shaking).

Was it a hospital bed? It felt thin and...contingent, like those beds do. Contingent on the fact of illness. On something being wrong.

Something *was* wrong.

I felt around for a lamp beside my bed. Felt around for my glasses, but they weren't there. My mouth tasted metallic, tasted of green pennies. I recognised the curdled feeling in my veins. I'd taken something. Been given something. I found the lamp and switched it on.

A cold light flooded the room. It was a big dormitory room, long and white and narrow, with six beds to the left, five to the right, and my own bed at the end, under the window. There were people in the other beds; I saw lumps and shapes rising from the pale green blankets. Children, I thought, because the shapes were so small.

This was all…this was all so familiar. I'd been here a long time. Strapped to the bed, thick syrup of drugs in my veins, nice and sleepy. Only I didn't like the dreams, the dreems, the dreams…they were terrible. But all I had to do was wait for morning and Doctor Lumna would be there to take my pulse and hand me my tablets in a little white cup. And Tom would visit, and my mother…my mother…something about my mother I couldn't remember. They would have to tell me again. Whatever it was. Tom would have to tell me. He would have to visit and sit on the bed and tell me stories in his sleepy voice; that was how I lived now.

There was a strange, sparkly feeling in the air. And in the other beds, movement. The bodies were wriggling, thrashing around. And they sat up, one by one. Perfectly smooth plastic skin and curls and rosebud lips. Mechanical giggles as they got out of bed in their stiff frilly dresses. I got out of my bed, too. I was wearing the black satin puffed sleeve dress and black satin shoes. I put a rubbery numb hand to my face. Like a doll, touching.

The others began softly singing in robotic harmony.

it's a dreemy world, living in a dreem
our hearts are made of plastic
a dreemy world where none of us are real
our heartstrings are elastic
we are dreemers living in a dreem
and we don't feel a thing
but we dance all night in the silvery moonlight
to the songs of the cully king

The song began again as soon as it finished and I found myself humming along; the melody was so dreamy and lilting like fairground music or a nursery rhyme. I found it tranquillising, comforting. My hands and arms were numb and that was fine. We didn't feel a thing.

I followed the others to the middle of the room where a trapdoor opened. The steps went down in darkness. I was running my hands along the bare stone walls. They were wet and mossy and studded with tiny sparkling snails. *Into the under-the-house.* I heard music, faintly, from below. A familiar melody. Down we went, down and down, our voices singing in unison.

we are dreemers living in a dreem
and we don't feel a thing
yes we dance all night in the silvery moonlight
to the songs of the cully king

A dim light spread up from below. The stairs gave out into a wood, where the trees were made of crystal, and the forest floor was strewn with glistening rocks and gems.

it's a dreemy world, living in a dreem

We sang. I waited for the loudest part of the song

we are DREEMERS living in a dreem...

and snapped a crystal twig from a tree as I passed by underneath. It rang out and the woods quivered. But my sisters kept on singing and we walked on, in our awkward trundling way, through crystal woods, and woods of silver and gold, until finally we came to a broad black lake, with a crystal castle glittering on the other shore, and twelve white paper boats bobbing in the water. I thought we were too big and the boats too little and weak to carry us over the lake.

But as we'd been walking we'd grown very small and now the boats were the perfect size. Each one was complete with an oarsman to row us across.

My sisters each chose an oarsman and a boat, and they set off in smiling pairs, over the black lake, under the light of the stars gleaming on the crystal forests. There was one remaining boat and oarsman. He was clothed in black velvet with a diamond drop in his ear, and diamond buckles on his shoes. I knew him, and felt confused.

We stepped into the boat and he began to row us after the others. Now I heard the dreemy music playing over the water. My sisters' voices singing. Mine too.

and we don't feel a thing...

It was a dreemy world, it really was. The oarsman was dreemy, the music, the castle, the dancing; even the water was dreemy. I couldn't feel anything; the boat was gliding through the lake with no friction or effort. There were barely any feelings left in the world.

But the oarsman said, "Doesn't the boat feel heavier than usual tonight?"

No, nothing was heavy. Everything was perfect and like a dreem.

But he was right. Now that he'd said it, I could tell there was something weighing us down. There was a hand reaching out of the water beside us. Another gripping the edge of the boat.

Then her head emerged. Caged in rusted iron. She was close enough that I could see the spike that went through her cheeks, the metal holding down her tongue. The terrible thing she had done to herself. She rose from the water and within a few strides she was at the shore. Despite her caged head, there was nothing mechanical or robotic in her movements. She was lithe and strode with muscular intention. She had power. I felt a little blue spark sizzle in my stomach. The oarsman startled.

Before the castle, he took my hand. "Don't eat or drink a thing!" he warned me.

But then we were in the ballroom, and the cully king was upon us.

%

The world was a dance and we were all dancing, spinning and whirling, our smiles open wide. A blur of faces, spinning, shining trails of glittery eyes. My ears rang from the loudness of the music. The cully king would not let me dance with anyone but him. He held me tightly against him, pressed to his greasy feathers. Every few moments he drew my attention to a table piled high with confections and cream cakes and pink fizzing sodas.

eat! drink! nothing is too much trouble!

I shook my head and the cully king whirled me around, again again again again

have something to refresh you, my dear!

We span by a table towering with marshmallows and a fountain of hot chocolate.

I whispered *no,* and he twirled me and span me dizzy. He was nothing but feathers, black feathers crawling with white lice.

do have a morsel, a nibble, a titbit!

"No thank you!" I said. Louder than I intended.

The music stopped. Everything came to a sudden halt and in the silence my ears were ringing like an alarm clock, like a hammer hitting a bell.

then let's get to business!

Time to tango, I thought.

"Time to tango," I said.

The cully king clicked his talons and scraped them on the ground.

you—

he pointed at two of the oarsmen

bring out the queen of cunts

I thought he meant my mother. And that this was another of his plays. But no, it was Rose they dragged out on her knees. Blood dripped from the cage around her head.

you fucking hag! ruined my fucking life!

The cully king screamed and kicked her between the legs. She crumpled over, trying to protect herself. He stamped on the ground in a rage. Then shook himself.

right, let's get on with it

Time to tango, I thought. Why was I thinking that. It was the same thing Tom said, that he said to me all the time. The cully king pulled me forwards so I was standing before Rose. She was bowed before me, her caged head hanging. I felt repulsed by her ugliness and madness.

you see rose, you see now rose, see who is writing this story? it's not you, is it rose? you thought you were so special but all the time you were mad! it's me, you see, i'm the one with all the ideas! the talent! the je ne sais quois, pardon my fucking french. and yet everything! always! had to be about you!

you can kill her now

He was saying that to me. You can kill her now. Why me, I wondered. It was true I had wanted to destroy her. She'd infected me with her madness and I wanted to wipe her out. I'd stalked her through the house and now I had her in my power. But she was pitiful. And I wondered why it had to be me? The cully king had no qualms about killing. He would kill Rose himself if he could. So obviously, he couldn't. He needed me.

I looked at him, full in the eyes, looking for the truth. He tutted and looked away.

did you bring your own weapon? no, well i suppose i have to do everything around here as usual. work my fingers to the bone for you, don't i? good job you're so swell!

He placed a pair of silver scissors in my hand.

%

"Let me help you," said Tom.

His hand closed around my hand, holding the silver scissors. His touch was all-encompassing; it was all there was in the world. *I love you*, I thought. Like my thoughts didn't even belong to me.

"You're beautiful, Anna," he said. "So beautiful. I know you don't think so, but you are. I want to prove it to you. Give me that chance."

His hand around mine was squeezing. The scissors were digging into my palm and my fingers. More than that, I felt the weight of his desire, pressing on me painfully.

"As long as she is allowed to go on, we'll never be happy.

Don't you want to be happy, Anna? I want to be happy. With you."

I wanted to be happy. I did. My vision cleared and I could see her again. Rose. On all fours, the cage of her head hanging down.

Tom was beside me. Around me. Inside me. His thoughts were in my mind. His fingers pushed between my legs. It was all for him. All for him. Because I loved him I loved him I loved him I loved him I loved him like a stuck record

a broken doll

reciting my lines and my limited language. Only the words I was allowed to say. Only the thoughts I was allowed to think. That and no more.

Rose's cage was a violation. A metal prison for her voice. She'd done it to herself. And me. I had done it to myself. I had let him make me dreemy. I had done it to myself.

"Anna. Please understand. I don't claim to be perfect. No, I'm a man – and we men, we are weak, we are driven by our desires. But I have been driven to you. I'm in love with you, Anna, and I don't care what anyone thinks, I don't care what the rest of the world says. Do you, Anna? Let's be together, and be happy."

His words spoke to the void in my soul. The empty place where I was unloved and unknown. He loved me. He would love me. That void was hungry. Starving. I wanted to stuff my face with his love, gorge on it, I'd do anything for it, anything. Get on my knees and suck the love out of him.

"I know it's asking a lot. But you *promised*. And once this thing is done, we'll be together. Nothing else can harm us. She'll be out of your head and you'll be you again."

Rose looked half-dead, anyway. Her strong lithe body crumpled. Her caged head hanging. The scissors were warm in my hand, my hand was numb and stuck. Tom's hand was on mine, cold and white and smelling of vanilla. Everything was leading up to the moment. The moment I destroyed her. For Tom. For Mum. For myself. I'd promised.

Rose was watching me now through the bars of her cage. And there was nothing else around us, no whirl of dance, no tower of cream cakes. It was only us, me and Rose and Tom. I was in a wide, cold, dark space. Out of time. I was falling down a deep dark well, falling and falling, so far and deep I'd forgotten I was falling, but I was. Down down down down. Rose's eyes were holding me there, mid-fall, in the middle of the air.

"You love me, don't you Anna?"

He wouldn't stop talking, I realised. He wouldn't stop and let me think. He would go on and on with his love talk, his sweet talk. On and on until I couldn't take it anymore, until I stabbed the scissors through Rose's chest. And I wondered. Why didn't he kill her himself? If that was all it took to make everything wonderful.

He needed me. The cully king needed me. And Tom needed me.

And Rose. She needed me too.

Tom squeezed my hand and made little thrusting motions, back and forth. "Just like that, Anna. Up and down. In and out. So easy and slick."

"Why does it have to be me?"

"It's an exorcism. She's possessed you. Now you have to free yourself."

I nodded. And felt him relax and release my hand.

"It's time," he said.

Time to tango, I thought.

%

do it, do it. dig in nice and deep

The Dreemy Peeple were whirling around us, dancing and filling their blank mouths with iced and frosted cakes, pink lemonade that frothed from their eyes and ears. They didn't pay attention to me or Rose or the cully king. All they could do was dance and dance.

Rose was on her hands and knees before me, watching me through her cage. Her face was monstrous, yes. But she did not seem mad.

The cully king, strutting around me: he was mad.

time to tango, he said.

I felt the little jolt and fizzle-out of a spell that no longer worked.

And *fuck you*, I thought. And I felt *my* spell landing. The cully king twitched and twittered, confused by the glitch in his enchantments. But still I closed my grip tight around the scissors, and knelt down before Rose. The cully king settled back into triumph. Rose was snarling, blood leaking from her mouth and the holes in her face. She was terrible, an ogre, the ugliest woman I'd ever seen. You did this to yourself, I thought.

No, you didn't.

The scissors felt like they were part of my hand. I knew that anything I did now had power. Would work. And for a moment, I rested in my power. They needed me. They were using me. Rose's eyes were shining with rage but she couldn't harm me. She waited, with a fierce and muscular impatience.

The lock in the metal was rusted and corroded. I wedged the silver scissors into the part of the metal which would give me the most purchase, and with three fast, twisting yanks back and forth, wrenched open the cage.

I know it hurt her. The pain must have been agonising. The nails drawing out of her flesh. Her tongue loosened and flowing with blood. She stifled a howl. She stayed on all fours, breathing hard.

oh excellent, you're going to put on a show

But his voice now was not so cocky, and he was backing away.

"You're scared," I said.

of that...snivelling thing?

It was true she was still on all fours, panting and heaving. But I could see she was gathering herself together. It would not be long now.

i thought you loved me anna! oh, oh you have broken my heart. I gave you everything you wanted! A beautiful house and wonderful clothes! You wanted to be beautiful so I made you beautiful! Beautiful and free from pain! Why is that so wrong?

"You gave me nothing. You took everything from me and gave me nothing. You didn't make me beautiful! You turned me into your puppet. Your Dreemy Peeple. Well that is not what I am."

what are you then? nothing but a little slut. remember what you did in the library? you loved it, didn't you? you couldn't keep your dirty hands off me. you begged me for it, you wanted it so bad, i nearly gave it to you. if you weren't so repulsive, such a dirty bitch. and now you think you can just walk away? you have SHIT FOR BRAINS you stupid ugly dirty little slag!

He was screaming at me now. His face morphing from feathers to flesh. He was Tom and the cully king. He was one and the same. And he hated me. He despised me. Even now, his words hurt. It hurt to know I meant nothing to him. That I was only his plaything for a while. But I knew the hurt was a passing thing. It would turn to anger. Like Rose had turned to anger. She had been so angry with him, so furious, he'd had to put her in a cage.

But now she was free. I sensed her gathering herself up behind me. Gathering her power. She drew herself up to her full height and then she kept on growing. Shooting up like a tree, shooting her roots down under the earth to where the soil was real and sustaining. I recognised her tree-ness, the hollow that had sheltered me.

And then she spoke.

%

She spoke and her speech was an undoing, an unravelling of the world. She spoke the world backwards, unspeaking an enchantment. She undid the castle, the shore and the lake. The crystal forest shook in a shiver of bells and burst into nothing. She unbuilt the house, she unwrote the books and started the clocks and shook the rain out of the clouds. Her words ripped through the void inside me. She spoke to unravel the spell and it dissolved in the rain.

It was one word, over and over.

No.

I was screaming. Over and over. Screaming into the rain.

We were not alone. There were others around us. But I was not conscious of anyone but him. *We were side by side in the mirror, his long white hand in the back of my hair...*

"No," I said. "No. That won't work anymore."

"Anna...what do you mean? I don't understand, darling."

"But you do."

He was touching my arms, running his fingertips along my spine. His breath on my neck.

"You're upset. You haven't been yourself lately. Come on Anna."

I became aware of Thew at my side. His mum, too. Others around me.

"I just. Want you. To keep my name out of your mouth."

Tom laughed. "What on earth is she – what on earth are you talking about, Anna? Good god. Is there a doctor here? I think we should get you home right away."

He hurried around the grave towards me, his feet sticking in the mud. I held up a hand. "No," I said.

"What do you mean, no? You love me, don't you, Anna?"

He was stroking the length of my spine. The fire was blazing.

"It's too late to say no. It hurts me. Don't you want us to be happy? I love you so much."

"No," I said, and all my heart was in that word. "Are you so stupid, you can't see? Your spell was nothing. It was all in my head."

"Yes, yes, that's right love. It's all in your head. You're seeing things and hearing things. We should get you back to the doctor. The stress, it's been terrible for you." He took a step towards me, but the others around me stepped closer too. "It's schizophrenia," he said to Thew's mum, who was in front of me now. She kissed her teeth.

"Oh Anna. This is really very upsetting."

His soft, understanding voice made me shudder. I remembered when I loved him, when I'd thought he was the only one who understood me, the one who would protect me. When I thought he was a genius, a great artist paying me special attention.

"You wanted to be beautiful, didn't you? You wanted to be loved. I loved you and made you beautiful and now you say it's not what you want at all. You make me so sad, Anna."

Side by side in the mirror. His long white hand, crawling in the back of my hair.

"I see things differently now," I said. "I can see another world, right behind you."

He looked surprised and glanced around. It was true: I saw now that all I had to do was turn my head and it was a different world. A world in which he was powerless over me. He looked so surprised, I almost felt sorry for him – almost, but not really. I allowed my voice to speak through me. *I am Rose,* I thought. *I am Sarah. I am all the women you've trapped and imprisoned, in photographs, in films, in cellars and sheds and bedrooms and in their own homes. In their own minds. All the girls you've manipulated and broken. All the children you made numb with your hate. But it ends here. It ends with me.*

He stumbled in the mud and slipped to his knees. He was so pathetic, now, so weak without a woman or a girl propping him up. I saw him try to laugh but he couldn't bring himself to do it. But I laughed: my body surged with strength and power. It was undeniable, and there was nothing he could do about it. He clutched himself and cried. A black cloud beat around his head. He tore at the air, tearing wings, blood and feathers flying.

///

I stood in front of the mirror and it broke. The air cracked like glass, the ground splintered beneath my feet, the world fractured and fell away. The music that had wound through everything now gave way to a symphony of crashing glass, and silence.

And me, then, I was alive. I rose inside myself like a volcano, the earth cracking open, the hot core pushing out. I felt my own power rising up inside me, my own voice. Uncaged and free and insistent and wild. And in my voice was all my strength, everything that had been stolen from me, everything I had given away. All that I had done, all that had been done to me. My dreams invaded. My body violated. My heart broken. I had withstood it all, taken it all into myself and now – now I let it all go. And I roared.

I *felt* the spell breaking around me; I saw the brittle veneer shatter and fall away, raining shards into the ground. The dark sky broke. I watched Tom die, saw him run out of himself, a dwindling oily shadow.

Look at him. He was nothing without me. By himself he was nothing. Only a mirror, reflecting back desire. He lived from others like they were food; draining their blood and sucking on their bones. Without us, he was nothing. Without those women he so despised, the children he played his cruel games with, he could not even live. It was the most pathetic thing I could imagine.

Everything he'd done, all that he'd put us through: it was all in the service of an illusion. That he was brilliant and unique. That his love was a precious rare gift. That he was the cully king, the king of birds, and his hands were full of terrifying magic.

As if we could ever be afraid of such a greasy little crow. Peck peck pecking around.

I ran from the house as it shrivelled around me. It shrank to one dimension and grew small and derelict. I stumbled through the back door and skidded and slidded down the garden towards the woods.

Time had begun again; it was the middle of the night. I could feel time flowing through me as I ran and pushed myself through tangled bushes into the woods. My fingers stung with cold. My trainers were two hard, misshapen, water-ruined lumps. A cold vein trembling under my skin. But adrenalin was still sprinting through my veins. I was shaking. It was over, all over. Tom was dead. I hoped he was dead. I knew he was.

My mother was long dead, buried in the ground. I could not begin to think of her yet.

And Rose. She was the only one who never believed in the dreem. He had to nail down her tongue to stop her from speaking. Now I knew why. When I set Rose free, the truth she unleashed had set us all free. The others, the other girls, the Dreemy Peeple... It hurt me to think of how I'd hated them, how I'd despised their perfect little faces. Now I understood we were the same. Lonely little girls. Taken out of school. Trapped in mirrors. Made to live on dreams and air. Made pretty and stupid and silent. It hurt so much to stop dreeming. But even so I was glad. Glad because they were no longer trapped in numb unfeeling fantasy. Because now their souls were free to roam. I hoped they would wander on; that they would be born again or settle into a glorious unity. I hoped it still meant something to be free. And I considered what I owed them. They could never tell their stories. But I could. I would.

%

That night I curled up in the hollow of the tree. I dreamed or I did not dream. It seems to me now, by the light of many years later, that it was not a dream but a vision of the real. A fox came into the hollow. She came close, unthreatening and unafraid, and sniffed the air around me. Tilted her ears. Curled her long beautiful thistle of a tail, coarse earth-red brush tapering to white. I held my breath, drank in the sight of her. Her fox eyes the colour of dark amber, flecks of gold moving in the deep. A chime, a star dropped into dark water. She lowered her head, sniffed my neck. Hot breath on my skin. Her own scent like wild, darkling woods. She circled in the hollow, brushing against my legs. Her belly was soft from all her litters. She lay down, curled around my feet.

With trembling hand, I stroked her earth-red hair, her fine-bristled ears, the soft fur under her neck, curling into her breast. Touched a scar, deep in her shoulder, healed now.

A more recent notch across her nose. But nothing diminished her. The smell of her, the way she belonged to herself, how she lived in every cell of herself. The weight of her body warmed me. Glowing, from my feet through my whole self.

There is other magic. The kind that lives in the hollow of a tree, the kind that is in the tail of a fox. I remembered Thew, running down the fire escape in the rain. His body flaming into fox's body. In the morning, or sooner, he would come. And the work of telling would begin, and never end. But first I would sleep in the hollow, with the fox resting her warm weight upon me. For a time we were wild creatures, sleeping in a nameless wood.

And the wild free life, that had never really stopped, began again.

ACKNOWLEDGEMENTS

Thanks to Andy Cox for taking on this book and sticking with it, rewrites and annoying typefaces and all. Thanks to Vince Haig for the genius cover art. Thanks to Priya Sharma for her unwavering support through the painful process of imagining the story. Thanks to Penny Jones and Henry Szabranski, brilliant first readers who helped steer the book to its destination. Any mistakes that remain are entirely my fault. Thanks and squawks to the Bird King from the Cully King. Thanks to the many writers I am privileged to call my friends, for their honesty and kindness. Thanks to Judy Smart for her compassion. Thanks to the powerful women in my life who are carving their own paths out of nothing but their need to get somewhere. Thanks and love to everyone who knows this house and its horrors. Thanks also to me. Thanks to foxes, crows and trees. Thanks to the wild free life that never ends.

ABOUT THE AUTHOR

Georgina Bruce is the author of a collection of stories, *This House of Wounds* (Undertow Publications). Her short story 'White Rabbit' (*Black Static* issue #50) won the 2017 British Fantasy Award for Best Short Fiction. She lives in Edinburgh where she works as a teacher.

TTA NOVELLAS

1: Eyepennies by Mike O'Driscoll (sold out)
2: Spin by Nina Allan (sold out)
3: Cold Turkey by Carole Johnstone (sold out)
4: The Teardrop Method by Simon Avery
5: Engines Beneath Us by Malcolm Devlin
6: Honeybones by Georgina Bruce

Available from shop.ttapress.com